USBORNE FIRST READING
Level Four

USBORNE FIRST READING

Why the Sea is Salty

Retold by Rosie Dickins
Illustrated by Sara Rojo

USBORNE FIRST READING

The Reluctant Dragon

Based on the story by Kenneth Grahame
Illustrated by Fred Blunt

USBORNE FIRST READING

THE EASTER STORY

RETOLD BY RUSSELL PUNTER
ILLUSTRATED BY JOHN JOVEN

USBORNE FIRST READING

Thumbelina

Retold by
Susanna Davidson
Illustrated by Petra Brown

Jack and the Beanstalk

Retold by Susanna Davidson

Illustrated by Lorena Alvarez

Reading consultant: Alison Kelly

Jack and his mother lived in a shabby old house.

They had shabby old clothes
and very little food.

"We'll have to sell Milky-White," said Jack's mother, "or we'll starve!"

Poor Milky-White.

"Today's market day. Take Milky-White and get the best price you can."

Moo!

"I will," promised Jack.

But on the way, Jack met
a strange little man.

The man danced down
the path, whistling a
strange little tune.

"Where are you going?"
asked the little man.

"To market, to sell my cow,"
Jack replied.

"I'll buy her," said the little man, "for five beans."

"Beans!" scoffed Jack. "I don't want beans. I want money."

"Ah!" said the little man.
"But these are *magic* beans.
Plant them tonight...

...and tomorrow you'll have a beanstalk that touches the sky."

"That's incredible!" said Jack, handing over Milky-White.

And he ran home, clutching
his bag of beans.

But when he got home he was
in trouble – big trouble.

"We need money, not beans,"
cried his mother. "What are
we going to do now?"

12

Angrily, she hurled
the beans out of the
window.

Jack went to bed without any supper.

His tummy rumbled
with hunger.

He felt sorry for himself.
He felt sorry for his mother.

At last, he cried himself
to sleep.

The next morning, his room
felt different.

It was dark and dingy.
Leaves covered the window.

"A beanstalk!" cried Jack.
"The beans have grown."

The little man
was right!

The beanstalk was so tall it
touched the sky.

"I wonder where it goes?"
thought Jack.

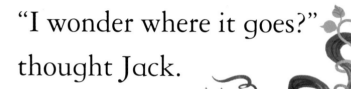

And he began to climb.

18

Up, up, up he went.

There, at the very top, was a
castle in the clouds.

On the doorstep stood an
enormous woman.

"A giantess!" gasped Jack.

"What do you want, little boy?" she growled.

"Please," said Jack, "may I have some breakfast?"

"You'll be breakfast if you don't go away," said the giantess.

"My husband loves to munch and crunch little boys."

"Please!" begged Jack. "I'm *so* hungry."

"Well, you'd better be quick," said the giantess.

She took Jack to the kitchen
and gave him giant-sized
crumbs of bread and cheese.

Then STOMP! STOMP!
STOMP! The whole castle
began to shake.

"Oh no!" cried the giantess.
"My husband's coming back."

"Hurry," she said. "You can hide in here."

And she picked Jack up and dropped him into a jar.

The giant strode into
the kitchen.

What's this I smell?

He stopped and sniffed the
air with his great hairy
nostrils.

"Where's my breakfast?"
he roared. "I want meat and
I want it now!"

29

"Fee! Fi! Fo! Fum!
I smell the blood of an Englishman,
Be he alive, or be he dead,
I'll grind his bones
To make my bread!"

"Nonsense dear," said the giantess.

"Perhaps you can smell the scraps of the boy you ate yesterday."

The giant began to wolf
down his breakfast.

"Now bring me my hen,"
he ordered.

His wife carried over the hen.
"Lay!" boomed the giant.

"She's laid a golden egg!"
Jack whispered.

The giant gazed at the egg for a while. Then his eyes began to close...

A moment later, he was fast asleep.

SNORE... SNORE...
SNORE...

The giantess plucked Jack
out of the jar. "Now's your
chance," she whispered.

"Run, Jack, run!"

But Jack had his eyes on
the hen.

He grabbed the hen and
dashed for the door.

The hen squawked in alarm.
It woke the giant...

...who jumped to his feet.

He roared when he saw Jack.

"A boy!" cried the giant.
"I'm going to eat him."
Jack jumped onto
the beanstalk.

SQUAWK!

The giant was just behind him. The beanstalk swayed from side to side.

"Mother!" Jack shouted as he climbed down.

"Fetch the axes!"

"What is that great big boot?" she cried. "Is it... is it... a *giant*?"

"Quick!" said Jack. "Help me chop down the beanstalk."

They hacked and hacked...

At last, the beanstalk came crashing to the ground.

Wheeeeeeeeeeee!

The giant flew through the air. He was never seen again.

45

As for Jack and his mother...

The hen laid a golden egg
for them every day.

They became rich beyond
their wildest dreams.

And Jack never ever climbed
another beanstalk.

About the story

Jack and the Beanstalk is an English fairy tale. The oldest known written version dates from 1807, but the story was around long before then. The cry "Fi, fo, and fum!" also appears in William Shakespeare's play, *King Lear.*

Designed by Laura Nelson
Series designer: Russell Punter
Series editor: Lesley Sims

First published in 2015 by Usborne Publishing Ltd.,
Usborne House, 83-85 Saffron Hill, London EC1N 8RT, England.
www.usborne.com Copyright © 2015 Usborne Publishing Ltd.